ZATHURA

ZATHURA™

DELUXE MOVIE
STORYBOOK

Adapted by
DAVID SEIDMAN

Screenplay by
DAVID KOEPP & JOHN KAMPS

Based on the book by
CHRIS VAN ALLSBURG

Produced by Intervisual Books, Inc.
Houghton Mifflin Company, Boston 2005

www.zathura.com

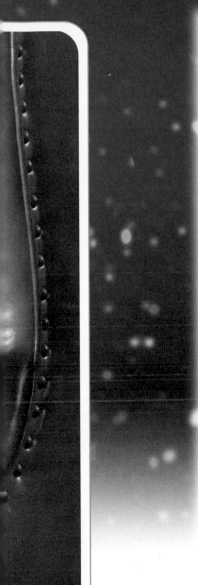

"Do you want to play a game?" Danny asked his older brother, Walter.

"No. You'll cheat," Walter said, his eyes fixed on the TV.

"How 'bout if you and me play catch?" Danny asked.

"It's 'you and I,' and no, I won't play catch with you."

Danny tossed his baseball at Walter anyway, and hit him in the head.

"You're DEAD, Danny!" Walter shouted as Danny ran upstairs. Their older sister, Lisa, was asleep in her room. She was used to her brothers fighting and slept right through it. Danny hid in a dumbwaiter—a little elevator on a rope.

"Daaaannnnyyy . . . " Walter called as he came closer to the dumbwaiter. "You're not still scared of the basement, are you?" Walter let go of the rope and the dumbwaiter dropped to the basement.

The basement was pitch black, except for a few small beams of light coming through the storm cellar doors. Danny looked around at the musty piles of junk that had been there since their Dad bought the house.

"This place looks creepy," Danny thought. He shot out of the dumbwaiter and ran for the stairs.

But before he reached the basement door, something caught his attention. Under the stairs, a ray of light shone on an old box with a picture of a rocket and the words "ZATHURA: A Space Adventure."

"Check out what I found in the basement," Danny said, forgetting he had been running from Walter a minute ago. Walter's eyes didn't move from the TV.

Danny opened the box. Inside the box was a board game with a path of circles from Earth to a black planet called Zathura. Two spaceships, one red and one blue, poked up near Earth. There were other things too—a dial with numbers, a button to push, and a key like the ones that run wind-up toys.

Danny turned the key and pushed the button. The dial spun. It stopped on FIVE, and the red ship jumped five spaces! Suddenly, a card popped up from the board. It said, "Meteor shower. Take evasive action."

"What's 'evasive action'?" Danny asked.

"It's when you get out of the way of something." Walter replied.

At that moment, flaming space rocks started raining through the ceiling! Danny tried to run, but the rocks followed him. Walter hid in the living room's fireplace, so Danny crammed in there, too. That's when the storm stopped, as if it had been waiting for them to do what the card said.

The boys slowly crept out of the fireplace and looked around at the smashed, smoking living room.

Then, they looked up.

Through the holes in the roof, the boys could see a black sky dotted with stars. They were looking at a nighttime sky, but it was afternoon.

"Wow. Outer space!" Danny said.

The boys woke their sister, Lisa.

"If this is a joke, I swear you're dead," she said. To show her how the game worked, Walter pushed the game's button. The blue spaceship bumped forward, and a card popped up. It said, "You are promoted to Starship Captain." Nothing else happened.

"Fascinating," Lisa said. She went into the bathroom, started the shower, and shut the door.

"That one didn't count!" Walter shouted. Danny then took a turn. The card said, "Shipmate enters cryonic sleep." All of a sudden, they felt a draft of cold air coming from the bathroom.

"Does 'cryonic' mean 'ice'?" Danny asked as he opened the bathroom door.

The bathroom tub looked like a skating rink. The shower water looked like long icicles, and Lisa was covered in frost.

"We gotta do something," Walter said. "What did the game's rules say?" Danny ran to get the game box.

"There is no turning back until Zathura is reached," Walter read aloud. "Pieces reset at the end of each game." If the boys wanted to get back to normal, they had to play to the end.

"When we play the game, bad things happen," Danny said, but Walter pushed the button anyway. His blue spaceship moved forward, and he got a card that read, "Your robot is defective."

Clank-clank-clank. The boys heard a strange sound coming from the living room.

A small metal robot came in the doorway. "Alien life form," it said, with its eyes fixed on Walter.

Walter wasn't worried, until . . . the robot started growing . . . and growing! "Must destroy," it said, launching itself at Walter.

"**Q**uick, Danny, go!" Walter shouted. "It's your turn!" Shaking with fear, Danny punched the game's button. The red spaceship moved forward. Up sprang a card.

"Pass close to Tsouris-3," Danny read. "Gravity increased." The game slid toward the front window. The boys felt something pulling them in the same direction. Out the window, they saw a big orange planet, which could only be Tsouris-3! Its heavy gravity pulled on curtains, books, and everything else—including Walter and Danny.

Walter wedged himself into a doorway to keep the planet from pulling him out of the house, but now he was a perfect target for the robot.

The robot jumped at Walter, but Tsouris-3's pull sent the robot flying past him and through the doorway to the basement! Walter was safe, but Danny was barely holding on to a light fixture.

Fortunately, Tsouris-3 slipped away. Gravity went back to normal. Walter found the board and took his turn. Up popped a card that said, "You are promoted to Fleet Admiral," but nothing else happened.

Danny took his turn again. "You are visited by Zorgons," said the card that sprang up.

"That doesn't sound so bad," Walter said. "Visitors is all. What's a Zorgon?"

Then . . . SCREECH! SCREECH! The boys covered their ears.

A dangerous-looking spaceship pulled up alongside the house, and it pointed a cannon at the boys! These visitors were not friendly.

"Hide!" Walter shouted, but before they could move, the cannon shot fireballs through the house.

Walter grabbed the game from Danny and pressed the button. He got a card that said, "Reprogram." He pushed the card at the Zorgon ship, but they fired again.

"It doesn't work!" Danny yelled.

Walter shoved the card into his pocket and shouted, "Spin!"

Danny smacked the button and got a card: "Rescue stranded astronaut." Just as he finished reading the card, a scruffy but tough-looking man in a space suit slammed through the front door.

"Turn off the lights," the astronaut instructed Danny. To Walter, he said, "Kill the pilot light on the stove."

As the boys did what they were told, the astronaut set the living room couch on fire!

"Open the front door!" he yelled at Danny. He turned to Walter and shouted, "Give me a shoulder!" They shoved the sofa through the door and into space.

"Zorgons are like lizards. They're heat-seekers," the astronaut explained. Sure enough, the spaceship flew after the burning couch. "The real problem is they never stop eating meat, and . . . YOU'RE meat."

"Let's just finish the game," Walter said.

"All right," the astronaut said. "Whose turn is it?"

But as they sat down around the board, Walter didn't like what he saw.

"I was ahead of you, Danny," Walter said. "You cheated! My red spaceship was ahead of your blue ship!"

"Easy guys, easy," the astronaut said. "Did you move the piece?" he asked.

"Maybe it moved by accident," Danny said quietly.

Walter tugged his ship past Danny to make the game fair again, but as he did, up popped a card: "Caught cheating. Automatic ejection." Walter shot toward the ceiling like a missile and flew through the roof!

"Throw me something with a cord and pull me down!" he shouted as he held on to the edge of the house.

Danny threw a lamp at him, but it hit Walter's head and floated away.

"Ouch!" Walter yelled.

The astronaut flew up, using his jetpack, and pulled Walter down.

"Why did the game punish me?" Walter asked as his feet touched the ground. He got no answer, so he said, "Let's just play so I can get away from him."

"I told you I was sorry." Danny said as he took his turn: "Go back two spaces."

Walter took a turn next. "Shooting star," said his card. "Make a wish."

"That's gotta be the best card!" Walter shouted.

"Make your stupid wish," Danny said. "I don't care."

"That's 'cause you never win at anything! You cheat all the time!" Walter shouted. "And you almost got me killed!"

"I don't care if I did!" Danny shouted back, and threw the game at him.

Danny ran upstairs.

"Don't do it, Walter," the astronaut said. "Don't wish what you're thinking."

It was too late.

"Danny?!?" The astronaut shouted as he ran up the stairs, three at a time. There was no answer. He threw the door to the boys' room open, and no one was inside.

"You have no idea the life of misery you've brought upon yourself," the astronaut said. He turned on Walter and shook him. "How could you do that to him?"

"Leave him alone!" Danny yelled, crawling out from under the bed.

The astronaut looked confused and relieved. He had thought that Walter had wished Danny away, but Walter had only wished for an autographed football.

"Twelve years ago, I played this game with my brother," the astronaut explained. "We were fighting a lot. I landed on the star space. I wished my brother had never been born. I've been inside the game ever since, looking for a way to get my brother back." He wiped his forehead. "Is it getting warm?"

The boys didn't answer, because they heard wood cracking, metal screaming, and glass shattering. The Zorgons were back and tearing off part of the living room.

They all knew the only way to stop the Zorgons was to finish the game, but the game was downstairs in the living room, and the Zorgons had it!

"Oh, no!" It was Lisa, coming from the bathroom. She had thawed out and turned up the house's heat, which had brought the Zorgons back.

"I'm going to get the game," the astronaut said. Danny, Walter, and Lisa hid behind a door. A few minutes later, they heard heavy footsteps coming closer. The door slammed open.

It was the astronaut!

"The game is in the basement," he whispered. "I couldn't get it. Too many Zorgons."

"The dumbwaiter—that sliding-doors thing—you could sneak down in it and grab the game," Danny said.

"That's a great idea, but I'm too big. I won't fit," the astronaut said.

They all turned and looked at Danny.

As Danny got into the dumbwaiter, Walter said, "Nothing's gonna happen to you, Danny. Because I'm your brother, and being a brother means I'll never let anything happen to you."

Walter carefully lowered the dumbwaiter. In the basement, Danny saw green Zorgon lizard-men shoveling junk onto a moving belt. The Zorgon ship hovered where a basement wall should have been. The belt was rolling toward the ship's furnace, and the game was on it! Danny snuck over, and just as it was about to fall into the fire, he grabbed the game and ran back toward the dumbwaiter. He tugged the dumbwaiter's rope to tell the others to pull him up, but the rope fell to his feet as though someone had cut it.

And now Zorgons were coming after Danny!

Danny ran for the stairway that went up to the living room. But the door at the top of the stairs was locked. A Zorgon tongue licked at the back of his neck.

Suddenly, the door flew open! Walter pulled Danny out of the stairway and locked the door.

"Told you I wouldn't let anything happen to you," Walter said. But how long would they be able to hold off the Zorgons?

Below, the boys could hear the Zorgons clawing at the basement door. Upstairs, they could hear Zorgons pounding toward them. Zorgons were everywhere!

The boys heard a horrifying sound in the basement, followed by a loud crash as the basement door blew into a million toothpicks.

The robot stood there. "Repair complete," it said. The robot must've fixed itself and taken care of the basement Zorgons. Walter and Danny cheered so loudly they almost didn't notice when the robot looked at Walter and said, "Must destroy."

"The card!" Danny shouted at Walter.

Walter fished a card from his pocket, pushed it toward the robot, yelling, "Reprogram!"

The robot turned to the Zorgons. "Must destroy."

The Zorgons spun around and hurried toward their ship, but the robot followed them and snuck on board right before the hatch closed. The ship flew off, twisting and turning as the robot attacked.

The boys called for Lisa and the astronaut, and they all went back to the living room to finish the game.

But the Zorgons must have called their friends. A swarm of Zorgon ships were flying toward them!

"What are you waiting for?" the astronaut said.

"Spin!" Danny took his turn and got a card that said, "Flunk space academy." BOOM! A Zorgon blast shook the house.

Walter hurried to take a turn. His card said, "Hit time warp. Go back three spaces and repeat last turn." Going back put him on the wishing star!

Sure enough, they saw a shooting star coming toward the house.

Walter whispered, "I wish the astronaut had his brother back." The star passed in a flash of light.

When it was gone, a kid who looked just like Danny was standing near the windows. He looked just as confused as everyone else.

The room was silent as he came toward Danny and touched Danny's hand. As soon as he touched Danny, he was sucked into Danny. They were the same person!

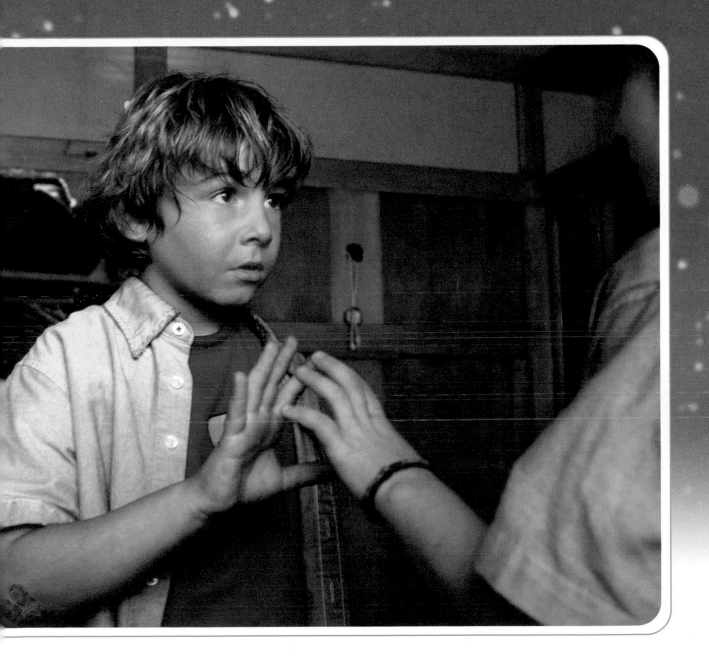

"You did good," the astronaut said. "You did better than I did." Then he touched Walter and got sucked inside him.

"He was . . . me?" Walter asked.

There wasn't time to think about it, because another Zorgon blast smashed a window and the front door.

It was Danny's turn. His red ship landed on the board's last space: the black globe called ZATHURA. The globe opened up, revealing something dark inside that swirled around and tugged Danny toward it. "It's a black hole!" Danny shouted. "Zathura is a black hole!"

Everything was being pulled toward Zathura. The books, lamps, and furniture went first. Then whole walls tore off and sailed into it. Lisa, Walter, and Danny went, too.

An instant later, the boys found themselves in the living room. Everything was in place, as if nothing had happened. Walter and Danny were sitting at the game board. The spaceships were where they had started, on Earth. They stared at the board, amazed.

"We did it!" the boys shouted. They grabbed each other and rolled on the floor, laughing.

No one would ever believe that they'd been on such a wild adventure—

"But you and me know, right?" Danny asked.

"You and me," Walter said.

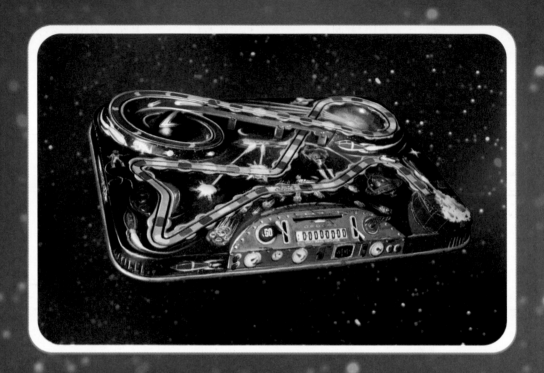